D0582469

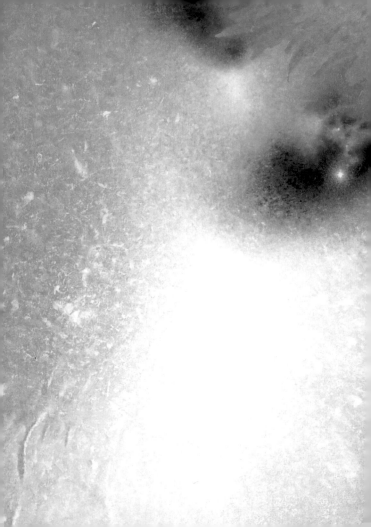

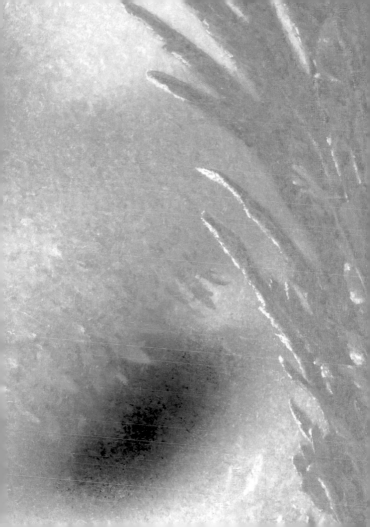

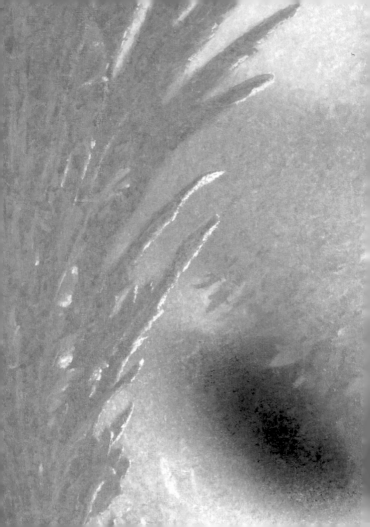

This is the star

For the newly born.
J.D.

To Lin.
G.B.

THIS IS THE STAR
A RED FOX BOOK 978 0 55 254883 0

First published in Great Britain in 1996 by Doubleday,
an imprint of Random House Children's Books

First Red Fox Mini Treasures edition published 2002

3 5 7 9 10 8 6 4

Text copyright © Joyce Dunbar 1996
Illustrations copyright © Gary Blythe 1996
Designed by Ian Butterworth

The right of Joyce Dunbar and Gary Blythe to be identified as the author and illustrator of this
work has been asserted in accordance with the Copyright, Designs and Patents Act 1988

Red Fox Books are published by Random House Children's Books,
61-63 Uxbridge Road, London W5 5SA,
a division of The Random House Group Ltd,
in Australia by Random House Australia (Pty) Ltd,
20 Alfred Street, Milsons Point, Sydney, NSW 2061, Australia,
in New Zealand by Random House New Zealand Ltd,
18 Poland Road, Glenfield, Auckland 10, New Zealand,
and in South Africa by Random House (Pty) Ltd,
Endulini, 5A Jubilee Road, Parktown 2193, South Africa

THE RANDOM HOUSE GROUP Limited Reg. No. 954009

www.kidsatrandomhouse.co.uk

A CIP catalogue record for this book is available from the British Library.

Printed in China

This is the star

Joyce Dunbar
illustrated by Gary Blythe

Mini Treasures

RED FOX

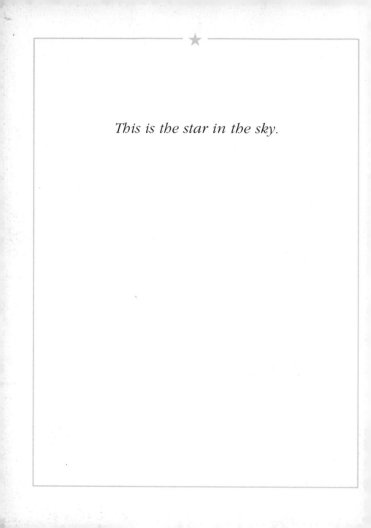

This is the star in the sky.

These are the shepherds watching by night
That saw the star in the sky.

This is the angel shining bright,
Who came to the shepherds watching by night
That saw the star in the sky.

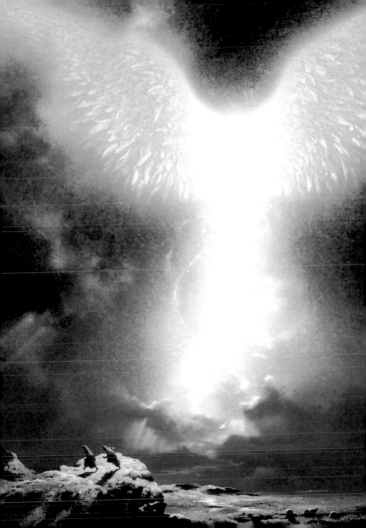

This is the donkey with precious load
Trudging the long and weary road,
Looked on by the angel shining bright,
Who came to the shepherds watching by night
That saw the star in the sky.

This is the inn where the only room
Was a stable out in the lamplit gloom
For the donkey and his precious load
Who trudged the long and weary road,
Looked on by the angel shining bright,
Who came to the shepherds watching by night
That saw the star in the sky.

This is the ox and this is the ass
Who saw such wonders come to pass
At the darkened inn where the only room
Was a stable out in the lamplit gloom
For the donkey and his precious load
Who trudged the long and weary road,
Looked on by the angel shining bright,
Who came to the shepherds watching by night
That saw the star in the sky.

This is the manger, warm with hay
Wherein a new-born baby lay.
This is the ox and this is the ass
Who saw these wonders come to pass
At the darkened inn where the only room
Was a stable out in the lamplit gloom
For the donkey and his precious load
Who trudged the long and weary road,
Looked on by the angel shining bright,
Who came to the shepherds watching by night
That saw the star in the sky.

This is the gold, and fragrant myrrh
And frankincense, the gifts that were
Placed by the manger warm with hay
Wherein a new-born baby lay.
This is the ox and this is the ass
Who saw these wonders come to pass
At the darkened inn where the only room
Was a stable out in the lamplit gloom
For the donkey and his precious load
Who trudged the long and weary road,
Looked on by the angel shining bright,
Who came to the shepherds watching by night
That saw the star in the sky.

These are the wise men come from afar
Who also saw and followed the star,
Bearing the gold, and fragrant myrrh
And frankincense, the gifts that were
Placed by the manger warm with hay
Wherein a new-born baby lay.
This is the ox and this is the ass
Who saw these wonders come to pass
At the darkened inn where the only room
Was a stable out in the lamplit gloom
For the donkey and his precious load
Who trudged the long and weary road,
Looked on by the angel shining bright,
Who came to the shepherds watching by night
That saw the star in the sky.

This is the child that was born.

This is the Christ child born to be king
While hosts of heavenly angels sing.
These are the wise men come from afar
Who also saw and followed the star,
Bearing the gold, and fragrant myrrh
And frankincense, the gifts that were
Placed by the manger warm with hay
Wherein a new-born baby lay.
This is the ox and this is the ass
Who saw these wonders come to pass
At the darkened inn where the only room
Was a stable out in the lamplit gloom
For the donkey and his precious load
Who trudged the long and weary road,
Looked on by the angel shining bright,
Who came to the shepherds watching by night
That saw the star in the sky.

Still shines the star in the sky.

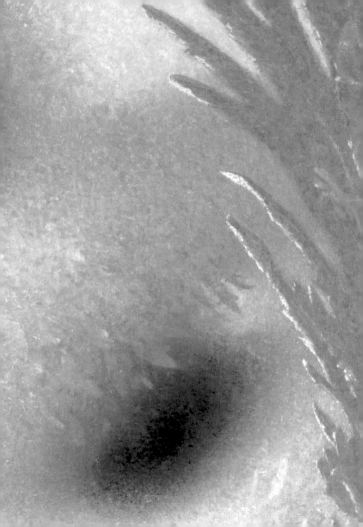